歐遊

何大文 著

記快

The Joys of Travel Europa

(By Diamante Ho

Forward
前言

During the outbreak of COVID-19, as I am unable to travel abroad for few years, I have time to sort out the emails to Mr. Martin, my good friend and former colleague with rich travel experience (we worked together in a "Fortune" 500 and one of the "In Search of Excellence" exemplary companies mentioned in the book), of which include between 2014 and 2019 my condensed "report" on the people's sentiments at the places I visited, and hope through this bilingual travelogue, I can share my experience of immense pleasure during these trips to Europe with the readers!

在新冠病毒疫情期間，由于我幾年無法出國旅行，因此有時間整理一下我給我的好朋友和具有豐富旅行經驗的前同事馬丁先生（我們曾在"財富"500強和"追求卓越"書中提到的典范企業一起工作）的電子郵件，其中包括 2014 至 2019 年期間濃缩地向他"匯報"我所訪問的地方的民情，并希望通过这本中英對照的遊記，能與讀者分享我在這幾次歐洲旅行中所經歷的無限樂趣！

This book called "The Joys of Travel Europa" is, of course, inspired by my beloved Qing Dynasty "Six Notes on Floating Life", and I also hope that it can be like the author Shen Fu who stated that: "So called famous places are what you feel about them, as some famous places are actually not very good, while some non-famous ones you find they are wonderful." Therefore, in my European tour from 2014 to 2019, the scenic spots and beautiful scenery are not important to me, as my focus is on visiting the city centres, shopping malls, taking public transportation, listening to the local tour guide's explanation of their people's feelings, etc. From watching the attitude of the local people towards life I learn their strengths, allowing me to correct my prejudices, just as Ming Dynasty painter Dong Qichang said: "If you can't travel ten thousand miles, you can't read ten thousand volumes of books, and you want to become paint master, how could you do so?"

　　這書名為"歐遊記快"，當然是套了我心愛的清朝 "浮生六記"而出來，也希望能如作者沈复般"名勝所 在，貴乎心得，有名勝而不覺其佳者，有非名勝自以為妙 者"。因此在我的 2014 至 2019 這幾年的歐遊中，名勝美 景對我並不重要，而把重點放在逛市中心、逛商場、乘坐 公共交通、聽當地導遊對民情的講解等，從觀察當地人的 生活態度學到他們的長處、修正自己的偏見，正如明朝畫 家董其昌所言："不行萬里路，不讀萬卷書，欲作畫祖， 其何得乎？"

　　Although I graduated from Hong Kong Baptist College (Business Administration), Louisiana Tech University (MBA), and Cornell University (Bachelor of Science - Mechanical Engineering), I found that despite reading 10,000 volumes of books, if I don't travel 10,000 miles, even at this internet age, I will still have serious ignorance of many situations and things
【Note: For example, in Song Dynasty General Yue Fei's "Man Jianghong" poem，the phrase of "Treading through and broken the valley of Helan Mountain", I used to wrongly believe the translation of this phrase as "Even Helan Mountain's pass to be flattened by my army's treading", until later when I came to Helan Mountain and realized this mountain is famous for its many passes. Even though Yue Fei has never been to Helan Mountain, he hoped by relating this phrase of going out of country's western border through all the different valleys of Helan Mountain many times (that is, "treading through and <u>broken</u> the gap in Helan Mountain" should be understood as "treading through <u>all</u> the gaps in Helan Mountains") to Mongolia to defeat the Huns, to metaphor his Yue family army's dozens of victories over the Northeast China Jin Dynasty】.

雖然我在香港浸會學院（工商管理）、美國路易斯安那理工大學(工商管理碩士)、和美國康奈爾大學（機械工程本科）畢業，但發覺儘管讀了萬卷書，如不行萬里路，即使在這個互聯網時代，我仍然會對很多情況和事情有嚴重的無知【注：例如宋朝岳飛將軍的"滿江紅"裡"踏破賀蘭山闕"，過去相信錯誤的翻譯為"連賀蘭山闕也要踏為平地"，後來到了賀蘭山，才知道這山以谷口多著名。岳飛雖然沒有到過賀蘭山，但是他希望能以多次通過賀蘭山所有（即"踏破賀蘭山闕"應該理解為"踏遍賀蘭山闕"）不同的山谷出塞西域蒙古去征服匈奴這詞，來比喻岳家軍數以十計戰勝東北的金朝】。

　　Moreover, while I was in Crete, I was quite distressed by the form of preserving thousands year old Knossos Palace after the excavation, hence, Chapter 7 is the paper I wrote about this monument during my university architecture class in the fall semester of 2019 【Note: this article has been reviewed and suggested revisions by this class' professor, TA, and 3 peer review group classmates】, and I hope readers can also resonate with my feeling about this situation

　　此外，由於在克里特島時我對超過千年歷史的克諾索斯宮挖掘後保存的形式感到很痛心，因此第七章是 **2019** 年秋季學期在大學上建築學課時對這古蹟所寫的論文【注：此文曾由這課的教授、助教、及 **3** 位評審小組同學等作出評論及修改建議】，希望讀者也能對這情況產生共鳴。

　　Meanwhile, naming the places where the writer visited is quite an issue. As this book involves many European countries, besides English is not the mother tongue for most of them, sometimes history (such as this book use Còrsegna and not Corsica or Corse, can be explained if you compare her flag with Sardegna), or popularity (more people know about Santorini than Thera) of these places have to take into consideration. As to translating the destination names into

Chinese, the writer has used the Mainland China's official ones. Besides they use correct pronunciation in local language, many of them incorporated the meaning of the destination's names (such as Hamburg's Binnenalster).

　　同時，對作者訪問過的地方命名是一個很大的爭論點。由於這本書涉及許多歐洲國家，除了英語不是大多數國家的母語外，有時還有這些地方的歷史（例如本書使用 **Còrsegna** 而不是 **Corsica** 或 **Corse**，這可以從她的旗幟與撒丁島的進行比較來理解），或者流行度（相比 **Thera**，更多人知道 **Santorini**）也要考慮進去。至於將這些地名翻譯成中文，筆者使用了中國大陸的官方地名。除了他們使用當地語言的正確發音外，許多地名還融入了目的地地名的含義（例如漢堡的內阿爾斯特湖）。

Finally, due to the e-mails included in this book are improvised, so in order to maintain the style, the content is presented according to the original text "without addition" as close as possible, and except for the one of me brewing Irish coffee in Dublin, all other photos in it are from the author's camera. Hence, I hope the readers can pardon me for any occurrence of mistakes and omissions.

　　最後，由於這書所包括的電郵是即興之作，因此為了保持文氣，內容盡可能按照原文"無添加"呈現，而除了在都柏林拍我調製愛爾蘭咖啡那張之外，其他所有的相片都是來自作者的照相機。因此，如有錯漏之處，希望讀者多多包涵。

Diamante Ho
何大文

Contents 目錄

5.0 Southern Europe 南歐

6.0 The Mediterranean Islands
地中海島嶼

7.0 Starting From Knossos
從克诺索斯開始
— **Reconstruction versus Conservation**
　　論古蹟應该重建或只是養護

1.0 British Isles 英倫三島

1.1 *England* 英格蘭

1.1.1 *Manchester, Liverpool* 曼徹斯特、利物浦
1.1.2 *Newcastle* 纽卡斯爾

1.1.1
Manchester, Liverpool
曼徹斯特、利物浦

Dear Martin:

Have arrived Manchester from Liverpool yesterday, and very happy (as shown in photo #A1) to find out that its National Football Museum (as well as other major museums), besides very interesting and well exhibited, it is also free!

昨天從利物浦到曼徹斯特，很高興（如照片#A1所示）發現它的國家足球博物館（以及其他主要博物館），除了非常有趣和很好的展示外，也是免費的！

Meanwhile, comparing to my last visit 30 years ago, Liverpool has made great progress to improve its dockyard (now a World Heritage Site)，as shown in photo #A2. Furthermore, I am surprised and excited that Liverpool's real estate price is very low, and with 40,000+ students (of 2 universities) accommodated in very small area right next to downtown, it may be a great investment opportunity!

與此同時，和我30年前的最後一次訪問相比，利物浦在改善其船塢（現已成為世界遺產）方面取得了很大進展，如照片#A2所示。此外，令我感到驚訝和興奮的是，利物浦的房地產價格非常低，並且有40,000多名學生（來自2所大學）居住在緊鄰市中心的非常小的區域，這可能是一項很好的投資機會！

M6227 - A1 (DSC02571)
Happy tourist at
Manchester National Football Museum
曼徹斯特國家足球博物館裡
的快樂遊客

M6227 - A2 (DSC02484)
Beautiful Liverpool riverside skyline
with the return of cruise ships
美麗的利物浦河畔天際線
與遊輪的回歸

1.1.2
Newcastle 纽卡斯尔

Dear Martin:

Referring to your e-mail, I agree with your feeling that the Scottish and English guides have different versions of the history of Great Britain! However, one thing is clear - the English exiled a lot of fierce and experienced Scottish warriors to America after the Battle of Culloden (1746), and no doubt, these Scots helped U.S. in the War of Independence!

有關您來的電子郵件，我同意您的看法，即蘇格蘭人和英格蘭人導遊對英國歷史有不同版本！然而，有一件事是明確的 —在卡洛登戰役（1746年）之後，英格蘭將大量凶悍且經驗豐富的蘇格蘭戰士流放到美國，因此毫無疑問，這些蘇格蘭人在獨立戰爭中幫助了美國！

Meanwhile, have arrived Newcastle from Edinburgh yesterday, and, as shown in photo #A1, I was quite impressed about Grainger's 450 buildings' transformation of Newcastle (1824-1841), with sewage system installed and combination of shopping & residential design, decades earlier than the important Paris and Barcelona Transformation! As to the sister bridge of Sydney Harbour in photo #A2, both of them were designed and built by the same team, i.e., by the time the Newcastle's bridge had been completed, the materials for Sydney Habour Bridge were still on the way to Australia!

同時，昨天從愛丁堡抵達紐卡斯爾，如照片#A1所示，格蘭傑對紐卡斯爾（1824-1841）的450棟建築物進行改造，安裝污水系統並結合購物和住宅設計，比重要的巴黎

12

和巴塞羅那的改造還要早幾十年！至於照片#A2所示的悉尼海港的姊妹大橋，它們都是同一個團隊設計與建造的，也就是說，紐卡斯爾的大橋建成時，悉尼海港大橋的材料還在運往澳大利亞的途中！

M6250 - A1 (DSC05341 & DSC05331)
Grainger Town of Newcastle
紐卡斯爾的格蘭傑城

M6250 - A2 (DSC05370)
Newcastle's sister bridge of
Sydney Harbour
紐卡斯爾的悉尼港姐妹橋

1.0 British Isles 英倫三島

1.2 *Ireland* 愛爾蘭

1.2.1 *Dublin* 都柏林
1.2.2 *Belfast* 貝爾法斯特

M6239 - Friday, August 26, 2016

Dear Martin:

Have arrived Dublin from Oslo two days ago, and as this year is centennial anniversary of Ireland Easter Rising, Dublin is full of revolutionary spirit, as shown in Photos #A1 - A2!

兩天前從奧斯陸抵達都柏林，由於今年是愛爾蘭復活節起義一百週年，都柏林充滿了革命精神，如照片#A1 - A2 所示！

M6239 - A1 (DSC04132)
Leaders of Easter Rising —
almost all executed by General John Maxwell
紀念復活節起義的領導人──
他們幾乎全部被約翰麥克斯韋將軍處決

M6239 - A2
(DSC04005)
Revolutionary
Tour Guide
宣揚革命的導遊

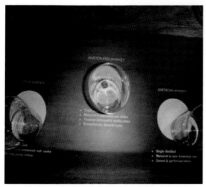

M6239 - A3 (DSC04132)
Tasting of Jameson,
12 Year Johnny Walker,
and Gentleman Jack
品嚐和比較尊美醇、
12年尊尼獲加、
和美國紳士傑克的味道

M6239 - A4
(DSC04158-2)
Making Irish Coffee
at Dublin
在都柏林製作
愛爾蘭咖啡

1.2.2
Belfast 貝爾法斯特

M6243 - Tuesday, August 30, 2016

Dear Martin:

Based on the observations from： (1) travelling between Dublin and Belfast (no passport control!); (2) passing small towns during the tour of Northern Ireland's Coastal Causeway; and (3) staying and travelling in Belfast, my feeling is Northern Ireland very likely will merge with the south in one to two generations' time, as the Catholics population has become the majority, and will win in future referendum. Hence, even though the countryside like Bushmills is still loyal to England, as shown in Photos #A1, however, Belfast now has many of her office buildings in Unionist sector empty!

根據以下三點：（1）在都柏林和貝爾法斯特之間的旅行（沒有護照管制！）、（2）前往北愛爾蘭海岸堤道時看到的小鎮、和 (3) 在貝爾法斯特市內逗留時的觀察，我的感覺是北愛爾蘭很可能會在一到兩代人的時間內與南方合併，因為天主教徒人口已成為多數，並將在未來的公投中獲勝。因此，即使像布什米爾斯這樣的鄉鎮仍然忠於英格蘭，如照片#A1 所示，但是大勢所趨，貝爾法斯特現在親英的民主統一黨區內的許多辦公樓都是空的！

M6242 - A1
(DSC04403)
Unionist Town of Bushmills
親英的民主统一党
布什米尔斯镇

M6242 - A2
(DSC04392)
Happy Tourist at
Northern Ireland
Giant's Causeway
在北愛爾蘭巨人堤道
的快樂遊客

M6242 - A3
Natural hexagonal columnar basalt at
Northern Ireland Giant's Causeway
北愛爾蘭巨人堤道之天然的六角形柱狀玄武岩

(DSC04384)

(DSC04390)

19

1.0 British Isles 英倫三島

<u>1.3 *Scotland* 蘇格蘭</u>

1.3.1 *Glasgow* 格拉斯哥
1.3.2 *Aberdeen, St. Andrews*
阿伯丁、聖安德魯斯
1.3.3 *Edinburgh* 愛丁堡

M6243 - Tuesday, August 30, 2016

Dear Martin:

Had a long trip (in one day experienced taxi/ferry/Cairnryan Border Control Posts/shuttle bus/train!) three days ago from Belfast across Irish Sea to Glasgow, as shown in photos #A1 to #A2.

三天前從貝爾法斯特穿越愛爾蘭海到格拉斯哥旅途很辛苦（一天內經歷了出租車—渡輪—凱恩瑞安邊境管制站—班車—火車!），如照片#A1 至 #A2 所示。

Due to limited time (I went to Scottish Highlands/Loch Ness for a full day to understand the feelings in Rabbi Burns's poem "My Heart..." which I have been familiar with since primary school), so in Glasgow I only visited the famous Glasgow School of Art Building — the mecca of Art Nouveau architecture (it was built in 1909, and severely damaged by fire 2 years ago, as shown in photo #A3) !

由於時間有限（為了解從我小學就熟悉的拉比・伯恩斯的詩《我的心……》中的感受, 去了蘇格蘭高地/尼斯湖一整天），因此在格拉斯哥我只參觀了著名的格拉斯哥藝術學院大樓 — 此處是新藝術風格建築的聖地（建於 **1909** 年，**2** 年前毀於大火, 如照片**#A3** 所示)！

M6245 - A1
(DSC04430)
***Ferry from
Belfast to Cairnryan***
從貝爾法斯特至
凱恩瑞安渡輪

M6245 - A2
(DSC04432)
Nice Seating on Belfastto to Cairnryan Ferry
貝爾法斯特至
凱恩瑞安渡輪上的
漂亮座位

M6245 - A3
(DSC04438)
Restoring Famous Glasgow School of Art Building
修復中的著名
格拉斯哥
藝術學院大樓

M6245 - A4
(DSC04621)
Loch Ness Urquhart Castle
尼斯湖
厄克特城堡

1.3.2
<u>Aberdeen, St. Andrews</u>
阿伯丁、聖安德魯斯

<u>M6245 - Thursday, September 1, 2016</u>

Dear Martin:

Have arrived Aberdeen from Glasgow yesterday, and visited St. Andrews (via Dundee) today. Considering its location at pretty northern part of Scotland, Aberdeen is growing quite well, as shown in Photo #A1.

昨天從格拉斯哥抵達阿伯丁，今天訪問了聖安德魯斯（經鄧迪）。考慮到它位於蘇格蘭相當北部的位置，阿伯丁的發展相當不錯，如照片#A1 所示。

As to St. Andrews, as shown in photos #A2 - A3, besides the golf, Kate and William also help to increase the fame of the University of St. Andrews, applications jump 30%!

至於聖安德魯斯，如照片#A2 - A3 所示，除了高爾夫球之外，凱特王妃和威廉王子也幫助提升了聖安德魯斯大學的知名度，申請入讀人數躍升 30%！

M6245 - A1
(DSC04725)
Very Modern Aberdeen Train Station Shopping Center
非常現代化的
阿伯丁火車站
購物中心

M6245 - A2
(DSC04821)
*Kate Middleton &
Prince William's
Alma Mater -
University of St.
Andrews*
凱特米德爾頓和
威廉王子的母校
聖安德魯斯大學

ML6245 - A3
(DSC04775 &
DSC04780)
*Happy Tourist at
St. Andrews
Royal & Ancient
Golf Club*
聖安德魯斯
皇家老球場
的快樂遊客

M6248 - Sunday, September 4, 2016

Dear Martin:

Had arrived Edinburgh from Aberdeen 2 days ago, and found this city even after summer holidays, was still full of tourists!

兩天前從阿伯丁到愛丁堡，發現這個城市即使過了暑假，依然遊人如鯽！

Moreover, during visiting 2 Highland whisky distilleries yesterday, had traditional Scottish dish, the Haggis, as shown in photo #A1, of which one Swiss tourist, who first asked the guide about it, could not 'stomach' it after trying it, but it was quite tasty to me!

此外，昨天在參觀 **2** 家高地威士忌酒廠時，品嚐了傳統的蘇格蘭菜哈吉斯（肉餡羊肚），如照片**#A1** 所示，其中一位瑞士遊客雖然首先詢問導遊這菜，但他嘗試後無法 "消化" 它，但對我來說卻很好吃！

Meanwhile, as shown in photo #A3, in both trips to Highland (Loch Ness and whisky distilleries), had passed through the important Stirling Castle, where Queen Mary of Scotland was born on December 8, 1542. My Scottish guide spent 30 minutes described how she was killed by her hypocritical first cousin, Elizabeth I of England, after more than 18 years' imprisonment. However, one thing I could not understand is the son of Queen Mary of Scotland, James I, can become the king of England, Scotland, and Ireland by inheritance from Elizabeth I!

與此同時，如照片**#A3** 所示，在兩次前往高地的旅行（尼斯湖和威士忌釀酒廠）中，都經過了重要的斯特靈城堡，蘇格蘭女王瑪麗於 1542 年 12 月 8 日出生於此。我的蘇格蘭導遊花了 30 分鐘描述了蘇格蘭瑪麗女王在被監禁 18 年之後，她是如何被虛偽的堂姐妹英格蘭的伊麗莎白一世殺害的。然而，有一點讓我無法理解的是，蘇格蘭瑪麗女王的兒子詹姆士一世卻可以繼承伊麗莎白一世成為英格蘭、蘇格蘭和愛爾蘭的國王！

(DSC04985)

M6248 - A1
Scottish Haggis -
Minced of Lamb's
Lung, Liver, & Heart
蘇格蘭哈吉斯 -
包含切碎後羔羊的
肺，肝臟 和心臟

M6248 - A2
Purchase
Cask Strength
Highland Single
Malt Scotch at
Deanston
在汀斯頓廠購買
木桶強度
高地單一麥芽
蘇格蘭威士忌酒

(DSC05011)

M6248 - A3
(DSC04959)
Stirling Castle
蘇格蘭
斯特靈城堡

2.0 Western Europe 西歐

2.1 *France* 法國

2.1.1 *Bordeaux* 波爾多
2.1.2 *Cognac* 干邑
2.1.3 *Reims* 蘭斯
2.1.4 *Dijon* 第戎
2.1.5 *Lyon* 里昂
2.1.6 *Cannes* 戛納

2.1.1
Bordeaux 波爾多

Dear Martin:

M9224 - Monday, August 9, 2016

After spending few days at Southampton/Portsmouth and Paris, enjoyed at Latin Quarter the best flan I have tasted (as shown in photo #A1，costs €2.50, same price as other French cities)，then arrived Bordeaux 2 days ago. Besides having very good time，as shown in the photos #A2-A4, very surprised that this "La Cité du Vin" is so cosmopolitan and still find so much British influence in it. No wonder Baron Haussmann, 18+ years of deputy prefect from this area, based on Bordeaux for his famous Paris Transformation project!

在南安普頓/朴茨茅斯和巴黎停了幾天，於拉丁區享用了我品嚐過最好的法式布丁蛋糕（如照片#A1 所示，費用 2.50 歐元,與其他法國城市的價格相同），然後于 2 天前到達了波爾多。除了如照片#A2 - A4 所示度過了愉快的時光之外，我并且非常惊讶这个"葡萄酒之城"是如此国际化及仍然受到如此多的英國影響。難怪曾在該地區擔任副長官超過 18 年的奧斯曼男爵，是以波爾多作為他著名的巴黎改造項目的基礎!

M9226 -Wednesday, August 14, 2019

During the 4 days in Bordeaux, have visited 6 "Classified" Château. Due to these winery tours are conducted mostly by the family members or senior management of the Château, besides having learnt quite a lot about wine-making (especially "la terre"), many questions in my mind from the time of my liquor store business were also fully answered!

在波爾多的 **4** 天裡，曾經參觀了 **6** 個有"等級"的酒莊。由於在參觀這些釀酒廠時主要是由他們的家人或酒莊的高級管理人員講解，因此除了知道許多有關葡萄酒制作的知識（尤其是"土壤的重要性"）之外，很多在我開酒舖時不明白的問題也得到了完全的答覆！

M9223 - A1 (DSC08332)
Coffee and Parisian Flan
at Latin Quarter
在巴黎拉丁區
享用法式布丁蛋糕與咖啡

M9223 - A2 (DSC06660)
With tour guide at
Bordeaux Place Royale
在波爾多皇家廣場
與導遊合照

M9223 - A3 (DSC06870)
Lunch At
Bordeaux Saint-Loubès
Château de Reignac
在波爾多聖盧貝斯
王朝酒莊享用午餐

M9226 - A4 (DSC06932)
Crémant de Bordeaux
At Saint-Émilion
Les Cordeliers
在聖愛美濃
科德利耶修道院
喝波爾多克雷芒起泡酒

<u>M9226 -Wednesday, August 14, 2019</u>

Dear Martin:

Have arrived Cognac from Bordeaux early this afternoon, and visited Hennessy factory afterwards. Even though the tour is well organized (including a short boat ride on La Charente), as shown in the following 4 photos, and the guide is very friendly, I am a bit disappointed as its approach is too modern, i.e., newly constructed visitor center with many nice videos, and except the cellar, no production facilities to be seen. May be visiting a smaller brandy manufacturer is a better choice!

今天下午很早就從波爾多到了干邑，之後參觀了軒尼詩白蘭地酒廠。儘管這次參觀組織得很有效率（包括在拉夏朗德河上乘船遊覽），見以下 4 圖，而且嚮導非常友好，但我還是有點失望，因為它的方法太現代化了，即雖然在新建的訪客中心有很多精美的視頻，但除了酒窖，看不到任何生產設施。可能去規模較小的白蘭地酒廠是更好的選擇！

M9226 - A1
(DSC07155)
Tasting VS &
VSOP Hennessy
Cognac
品嘗軒尼詩
VS 和 **VSOP** 干邑

M9226 - A2
(DSC07177a)
A Fancy
Hennessy Cognac
天價的轩尼詩干邑

M9226 - A3
Hennessy factory
轩尼詩白蘭地酒廠

(DSC07138)

(DSC07118)

M9233 - Wednesday, August 21, 2019

Dear Martin:

As shown in photo #A1, have arrived Reims from Dijon yesterday, visited Taittinger and Veuve Clicquot, and most impressed by the huge UNESCO listed limestone caves (stored millions of bottles, at 11 - 12 °C, no air-conditioning required) below these 2 wineries, as shown in photo #A2!

如照片#A1 所示，昨天已從第戎抵達蘭斯，參觀了泰亭哲和凱歌，印象最深刻的是在這 2 個香檳酒廠下面被聯合國列為世界遺產的巨大石灰岩洞穴（儲存了數百萬瓶，溫度為 11 - 12 ° C，完全不需要空調），如照片#A2 所示！

Meanwhile, as shown in photo #A3, the site of Taittinger was originally the Abbey of Saint-Nicaise which was destroyed at the time of the French Revolution. In the last 2 weeks, even after more than 200 years, the terror of French Revolution towards the destruction of the church (either severely damaged or destroyed) and monastery (monks were driven out, never returned) has keep repeating in Médoc, Saint-Émilion, Lyon, Burgundy, and Reims!

同時，如照片#A3 所示，泰亭哲香檳酒廠原為聖尼凱斯修道院，在法國大革命時期被毀。在過去的兩周里到梅多克、聖埃美隆、里昂、勃艮第、蘭斯等地，即使在 200 多年之後，法國大革命對教堂（嚴重受損或被毀）和修道院（僧侶被趕出，再也沒有回來）恐怖的破壞不斷重複地看到！

M9233 - A1　(DSC07980 & DSC08026)
Champagne tasting at Taittinger & Veuve Clicquot
品嚐泰亭哲和凱歌酒廠的香檳

M9233 - A2　(DSC07949)
UNSECO Site at
Taittinger Caves
位於泰亭哲香檳酒廠的
聯合國世界遺產洞穴

M9233 - A3
(DSC07988)
Taittinger built on
Abbey of
Saint-Nicaise
泰亭哲香檳酒廠
建立在
聖尼凱斯修道院
原址上

M9226 - A2
(DSC07177a)
A Fancy
Hennessy Cognac
天價的轩尼詩干邑

M9226 - A3
Hennessy factory
轩尼詩白蘭地酒廠

(DSC07138)

(DSC07118)

M6227 - Sunday, August 14, 2016

Dear Martin:

Have arrived Dijon from Lyon yesterday, visited Côte de Nuits and Côte de Beaune today, and very surprised to learn that Burgundy is so strict in the concept of "terroir", i.e., Grand Crus applied only to specific vineyard, usually at the middle of the slope, facing east, etc. Thus, as shown in Photo #A3, for Romanée-Conti, it can only come from that piece of land, so only have so many bottles can be produced, year after year, Pinot noir only, no blending with other grapes or nearby vineyards!

昨天從里昂到了第戎，今天參觀了夜丘和博讷丘，很驚訝勃艮第對"土壤"的概念如此嚴格，即列級酒莊只適用于特定的葡萄園，通常只限于那些在半山坡，面向東方等的葡萄園。所以，對於羅曼尼康帝來說，它只能來自照片#A1所示那塊土地，也只能生產這麼多瓶，年復一年，純用黑皮諾，并且不能與其他地區生產的葡萄或附近的葡萄園混在一起釀！

Meanwhile, have good time in taking the class of making as well as tasting Dijon mustard, as shown in photos #A2 - A3.

同時，很開心的品嚐了第戎芥末醬和參加了其製作班，如照片#A2 - A3所示。

ML9231 - A1
(DSC07812b)
At Côte de Nuits
Romanée-Conti
Vineyard
在夜丘
羅曼尼康帝
葡萄園

ML9231 - A2
(DSC07880)
Tasting Maille
Dijon Mustard
品嚐梅勒
第戎芥末

ML9231 - A3
(DSC07676)
Making
Dijon Mustard at
Edmond Fallot
在埃德蒙法洛廠
製作
第戎芥末醬

2.1.5
Lyon 里昂

M9229 - Saturday, August 17, 2019

Dear Martin:

    Have arrived Lyon from Cognac 2 days ago, and very surprised to find this city is both very scenic (with 2 rivers, Le Rhône and La Saône, joined at city center), and very modern, as shown in photos #A1-A2. And unlike London and Paris, it is very convenient and very low cost (about €1.3) to travel by **train** between Lyon's 2 main train stations, Part Dieu and Perrache!

    兩天前從干邑到達里昂，非常驚訝地發現這個城市既風景優美（有 **2** 條河流，羅納河和索恩河，在市中心匯合），又非常現代化，如照片#A1 - A2 所示。與倫敦和巴黎不同，乘坐<u>火車</u>往返於里昂的 _2_ 個主要火車站巴迪厄和佩拉歌非常方便且費用非常低（只需要 **1.3** 歐元左右）！

    Meanwhile, have taken local train (about 40 miles from Lyon) to experience what the Lyonnaise called the "third river of Lyon", i.e., the Beaujolais wines. As shown in photos #A3- A4, I have a very enjoyable day at the Michelin Green Guide 2 stars awarded Georges Duboeuf Winery, as the "King of Beaujolais" has turned his place into part museum of wine making, part Disneyland (with "4D" motion simulator ride and mini-golf next to vineyard), and part promotion of the beauty of the 40 square miles (almost all vineyards) Beaujolais area!

    同時，又乘坐地方支線火車去體驗里昂人所說的"里昂第三條河"，即博若萊葡萄酒區（距離里昂約 **40** 英里）。如照片#A3 - A4 所示，我在獲得米其林綠色指南 2 星的喬治•杜波夫酒莊度過了非常愉快的一天，因為"博若萊之王"已經將他的地方變成了一部分是釀酒博物館，一部分迪斯尼樂園（有"4D"運動模擬器遊樂設施和葡萄園旁邊的迷你高爾夫），還有一部分用來宣傳博若萊地區40平方英里（幾乎全是葡萄園）的美景！

M9229 - A1 (DSC07497)
World Heritage Vieux Lyon at the confluence of Rhône River & La Saône
在羅納河、拉索恩河合流
的世界遺產里昂老城

M9229 - A2 (DSC07576)
Modern Lyon Car Park with Michelin Green Guide One Star
取得米其林綠色指南 1 星
之現代化里昂停車場

M9229 - A3 (DSC07347)
Tasting Beaujolais at Georges Duboeuf Winery
在喬治・杜波夫酒莊
品嚐博若萊

M9229 - A4 (DSC07426)
Desert & Coffee Costs €7.50 at Michelin 1 Star Restaurant in Georges Duboeuf Winery
在喬治・杜波夫酒莊的
米其林 1 星餐廳
享用甜點與咖啡
只花費 7.50 歐元

2.1.6
Cannes 戛纳

Dear Martin:

Have arrived Cannes from Marseille yesterday, and was excited to find this town bustling with activities, as shown in the photo # A1. Unfortunately, when I returned from St. Tropez this Sunday evening, all the tourists had gone!

昨天從馬賽抵達戛納，興奮地發現這個城市熱鬧非凡，如照片#A1 所示。不幸的是，當我這個星期天晚上從聖特羅佩回來時，所有的遊客都走了！

Meanwhile, as shown in the photos #A2, have a pleasant day at St. Tropez, experiencing the jet setters playground's cost of living, like almost having € 12 per cup of Cappuccino at the famous Senequier Restaurant, but they did not have crepes. So I moved to its neighbour, a white tablecloth restaurant that serves crepes, and a cup of Cappuccino costs only €7.50!

同時，如照片#A2 所示在聖特羅佩度過愉快的一天，體驗一下這有閒階級樂園的消費水平，比如幾乎要化 12 歐元在著名的塞納基耶餐廳喝一杯卡布奇諾，但他們沒有法式薄餅。所以我換了去它的鄰居，一家有薄餅的白色桌布餐廳，一杯卡布奇諾只需要 7.50 歐元！

M5270 - A1
(DSC07846)
Tourists at
Cannes Le Suquet
遊客在
戛納老城區
勒蘇凱

M5270 - A2
(DSC07992 &
DSC07914)
St. Tropez Vieux
Port
sea of visitors and
Senequier
Restaurant
聖特羅佩老港口
遊客人海與
塞納基耶餐廳

2.0 Western Europe 西歐

<u>2.2 *Portugal* 葡萄牙</u>

2.2.1 *Porto* 波爾圖
2.2.2 *Lisboa* 里斯本

2.2.1
Porto 波爾圖

M5242 - Friday, September 11, 2015

Dear Martin:

Have arrived Lisbon on September 8, 2015, and after spending 2 nights, I rode the 3 hours long intercity train to the beautiful Porto São Bento Train Station (it took the artist 11 years to paint them on 20,000+ pieces blue and white azulejo, as shown in the photo# A1), and 1st class costs only €22.00 each way! Thus, Portugal gives me a very good feeling immediately for her capability to control the cost of living, like the cappuccino at Lisbon National Tile Museum costs only €1.00 and the cappuccino + Portuguese tart at Porto cafe viewing the Sé Cathedral costs only €1.50!

2015 年 9 月 8 日抵達里斯本，住了兩晚後，我乘坐了 3 小時長的城際列車到達了美麗的波爾圖聖本圖火車站 (藝術家用了 11 年的時間在 20,000 多件藍白瓷磚上繪製它們，如照片# A1 所示），一等座單程僅需 22.00 歐元！所以，葡萄牙對生活成本的控制能力立刻給我一種很好的感覺，比如里斯本里國家瓷磚博物館的卡布奇諾咖啡只要 1.00 歐元，而能看到波爾圖塞大教堂的咖啡館的卡布奇諾咖啡+葡撻只要 1.5 歐元！

Meanwhile, comparing to expensive wine tasting charges during my recent visit to Napa Valley, I am excited that Porto wineries let you taste a flight of Ruby, 10 Years Tawny, and 20 Years Tawny free of charge, as you can see from my happy face in the photo# A3!

同時，與我最近訪問美國納帕谷葡萄園期間昂貴的品酒費用相比，我很高興（從照片# A3 中我的笑臉可以看出來）波爾圖酒莊讓您免費品嚐紅寶石色、10 年茶色、和 20 年茶色一系列的波特酒！

M5242 - A1 (DSC05391)
Porto
São Bento Train Station
波爾圖
聖本圖火車站

M5242 - A2 (DSC05585)
Porto Bridge by
Gustave Eiffel
with structre quite similar
to the base of
his Paris landmark
居斯塔夫・埃菲爾造的
波爾圖大橋
結構與他巴黎地標
的底座非常相似

M5242 - A3 (DSC05554)
Flight of Port Tasting
at the Granham Lodge
在格蘭漢姆酒廠接待室
品嚐一系列波特酒

M5242 - A4 (DSC05736)
Douro Valley
Terraced Vineyard
杜羅河谷
梯田葡萄園

M5256 - Sunday, September 13, 2015

Dear Martin:

Have arrived Lisboa from Porto yesterday by train around 2:00 PM, and treated myself at Belem a "lavish" afternoon tea: McDonald cappuccino (€ 0.85 including tax) + 4 Pasteis de Beliem Portuguese tarts (€1.05 each including tax), as shown in the photos #A1 - A2!

昨天下午 **2:00** 左右乘火車從波爾圖抵達里斯本，並在貝倫為自己的享受喝了一頓 "奢華" 的下午茶：麥當勞卡布奇諾咖啡（含稅 **0.85** 歐元）＋ 4 個貝倫甜品店葡萄牙蛋撻（每個含稅 **1.05** 歐元）， 如照片#A1-A2 所示！

Moreover, have good times today！ As shown in photos #A3-A4, have travelled from Lisboa to Sintra (20 miles, by train), Sintra to Cascais (12 miles by bus), and Cascais back to Lisboa (20 miles by train), then took the ferry from Lisboa across the river and back, all these trips (including tram ride in Lisboa) together cost me only around €10 for a transport card and still got some money left!

此外， 今天有美好的時光！如照片#A3-A4 所示， 從里斯本出發到辛特拉（乘火車 **20** 英里）， 辛特拉到卡斯卡斯（乘公共汽車 **12** 英里）， 然後卡斯卡斯回到里斯本（乘火車 **20** 英里）， 再從里斯本坐渡輪越河到對岸來回， 所有這些旅程（包括在里斯本城內乘電車）只花了我約 **10** 歐元買的交通卡， 仍然還用不完！

M5256 - A1 (DSC05832)
*Queue for the Lisbon
most famous Pasteis de
Belém Portuguese tarts*
排隊買里斯本最著名的
貝倫甜品店葡萄牙撻

M05256 - A2 (DSC05841)
*Cappuccino & Belem Portuguese
Tart
at Belem McDonald*
享受咖啡與貝倫葡撻於
貝倫麥當勞

M05256 - A3
(DSC05860)
*Palácio Nacional
de Sintra*
辛特拉
國家宮殿

M05256 - A4
(DSC05974)
*Cascais
town center*
卡斯卡斯
市中心

2.0 Western Europe 西歐

2.3 *España* 西班牙
2.3.1 *Madrid* 馬德里
2.3.2 *Valencia* 瓦倫西亞
2.3.3 *Barcelona* 巴塞羅那

Madrid 馬德里

M5260 - Thursday, September 17, 2015

Dear Martin:

Have arrived Madrid from Lisboa 2 days ago, and visited the fancy office (as shown as shown in the Photos #A1) of your Georgetown University alumnus, Felipe Santos, yesterday morning. I am very impressed about his 2,800 rooms work place (he lives in the suburb), even more than Versailles and Hermitage. Unfortunately, Felipe is away on official business to Mexico and U.S. (and will visit his alma mater as well) this week, hence, I was unable to meet him!

2天前從里斯本抵達馬德里後，於昨天上午參觀了您美國喬治城大學的校友菲利普‧桑托斯的豪華辦公室（如圖#A1所示）。這2,800个個房間的工作場所（他家住在市郊）給我留下了深刻的印象，甚至超過凡爾賽宮和冬宮。很可惜的是，菲利普這週要出差去墨西哥和美國（也要去他的母校），所以我沒能見到他！

The next day, i.e., today, after a relax and late breakfast (around 11:15 AM, the hotel breakfast time is 7:30 AM to 11:30 AM - Madrid tempo is everything delayed by 2 hours!), I walked across the street to the Prado Museum, and spent about 3 hours quality time viewing 50+ Goya paintings, such as "Third of May, 1808" (plus a few of Raphael's masterpieces, including "the Cardinal").

第二天，即今天，在享用一頓優悠輕鬆的、很遲的早餐後（11點15分左右，酒店早餐時間是7點30分到11點30分 —— 馬德里的節奏是一切都延遲了2小時！），我步行到對街的普拉多博物館，並花了大約3個小時的高品

質的時光觀看了 **50** 多幅戈雅畫作，比如 "**1808** 年 **5** 月 **3** 日"（另欣賞拉斐爾的一些傑作，包括 "紅衣主教"）。

M5260 - A1
(DSC06260 &
DSC06277)
*Madrid Royal
Palace*
馬德里皇宮

M5260 - A2
(DSC06286)
Madrid Tapas
馬德里小吃

Valencia 瓦倫西亞

M5262 - Saturday, September 19, 2015

Dear Martin:

Have arrived Valencia from Madrid yesterday, and after few hours' walking from old town to the beach this afternoon, very excited to have finally reached Mediterranean Sea! To prepare for this "hiking" hardship, I have the famous Valencia Paella de Marisco for lunch, , and the afternoon coffee and luxurious McDonald macaron (possibly made by the sister company of Paris' Laduree) for afternoon tea, as shown in the photos #A1-A2!

昨天從馬德里到了瓦倫西亞，今天下午從老城區步行幾個小時到海灘，非常興奮終於到達了地中海！為了準備這"遠足"苦頭，我於中午吃了著名的瓦倫西亞海鮮炒飯，下午茶則是咖啡與奢華的麥當勞馬卡龍（可能是巴黎拉杜麗的姊妹公司做的），如照片#A1-A2 所示！

Meanwhile, have found Valencia's graffiti vandalism is not as bad as Madrid. In Madrid, almost all businesses suffer from graffiti vandalism (including window glass), and one restaurant has decided that "if you can't beat them, join them", as shown in the photo #A3!

同時，我發現瓦倫西亞的塗鴉破壞沒有馬德里那麼嚴重。在馬德里，幾乎所有的商家都遭到塗鴉破壞（包括窗戶玻璃），一家餐廳決定"如打不過他們, 就加入他們吧"，如照片#A3 所示！

M5262 - A1
(DSC06691)
The happy tourist and his Paella de Marisco near Valencia Mercado Central
在瓦倫西亞中央市場
附近的
快樂遊客和他的
西班牙海鮮飯

M5262 - A2
(DSC06748)
Coffee and macaron at McDonald near Valencia L'Oceangrafic
在瓦倫西亞
海洋公園附近
享受麥當勞的咖啡
和馬卡龍

M5262 - A3
(DSC06494)
Self-graffiti of a Madrid Restaurant
馬德里一家餐廳
的自我塗鴉

2.3.3
Barcelona 巴塞羅那

Dear Martin:

Have arrived Barcelona two days ago, and comparing to previous Valencia, I was shocked by the immense size of activities of this city, as shown in the Photos #A1 - A2. This feeling is quite similar to what I feel when I first visited Phoenix 20 years ago - I thought it was like Denver!

　　兩天前到巴塞羅那，和之前的瓦倫西亞相比，我被這個城市的活動規模之大所震撼，如照片#A1 - A2 所示。這和我 20 年前第一次去美國鳳凰城時的感覺很像—我以為它會像丹佛市那樣大小！

M5265 - A1
(DSC06704)
Very European style Valencia city center
極具歐洲風情的
瓦倫西亞
市中心

M5265 - A2
(DSC06983,
DSC07409
& DSC06926)
**Very NYC-like
Barcelona
city center & port**
非常像纽约市的
巴塞羅那
市中心和港口

3.0 Northern & Central Europe
北歐與中歐

3.1 *Sweden, Norway*
瑞典、挪威

3.1.1 *Stockholm* 斯德哥爾摩
3.1.2 *Göteborg* 哥德堡
3.1.3 *Oslo* 奧斯陸

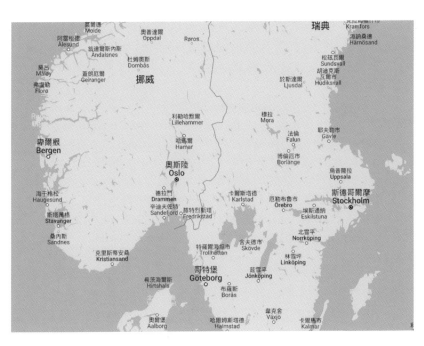

3.1.1
Stockholm 斯德哥爾摩

M6230 - Wednesday, August 17, 2016

Dear Martin:

Referring to your e-mail, even though I was crazy about soccer during my secondary school years in Hong Kong (my criteria in selecting the Grade 7 school was its two soccer fields!), however, I prefer American football - more fun to watch!

有關您的郵件，雖然我在香港讀中學的時候瘋狂的喜歡踢足球（我選擇中學的標準是它要有兩個足球場！），但現在我比較喜歡美式足球— 看得更有趣！

Moreover, have arrived Stockholm from Manchester yesterday, and surprised to find out there are so many tourists! In Vasa Museum (most visited in Scandinavia) this morning, being a student of leadership, I have to take a picture with King Gustav II, as shown in photo #A1. It is because due to his Royal Majesty's instructions to the engineers, the beautifully crafted 64 guns war ship "Vasa" sank after sailing only 1,400 <u>yards</u> during her maiden voyage in 1628!

另外，昨天從曼徹斯特到斯德哥爾摩，很驚訝發現遊客這麼多！今天早上在瓦薩博物館（斯堪的納維亞半島最多人參觀的旅遊點），作為研究領導能力的個案，我必須與古斯塔夫二世國王合影，如照片#A1 所示。這是由於在大帝親自對工程師的督工下，造工精美的 64 門火砲戰艦 "瓦薩號" 在 1628 年的處女航中僅航行了 1,400 <u>碼</u>就沉沒了！

M6230 - A1 (DSC02940)
Posted with Gustavus Adolphus the Great
at Vasa Museum
在瓦薩博物館與古斯塔夫・阿道夫大帝
合照影留念

M6230 - A2 (DSC02937)
The original "Vasa"
原來的"瓦薩號"

3.1.2
Göteborg 哥德堡

M6233 - Saturday, August 20, 2016

Dear Martin:

After arriving Göteborg from Stockholm yesterday, have very good feeling about this hometown of Volvo. It is because, besides many free cultural activities like dancing performance and concert during Sunday afternoon, Göteborg even has a very nice Tesla showroom (I found visitors were as excited as in Apple store), as shown in Photos #A1 - A4!

昨天從斯德哥爾摩抵達哥德堡後，對這個沃爾沃汽車的家鄉產生了很好的感覺。這是因為除了周日下午的舞蹈表演和音樂會等免費文化活動外，哥德堡還有一個非常好的特斯拉展廳（我發現參觀者和在蘋果店裡一樣興奮），如照片#A1 - A4所示！

M6233 - A1
(DSC03307)
Free Dance Performance at Göteborg City Center
哥德堡市中心
的
免費舞蹈表演

M6233 - A2
(DSC03330)
*Free Concert at
Göteborg
City Center*
哥德堡市中心
的
免費音樂會

M6233 - A3
(DSC03254)
*Excitement at
Göteborg
Tesla Showroom*
哥德堡
特斯拉展廳
令人興奮

M6233 - A4
(DSC03280)
*Inspecting Next
Generation Car
at Göteborg
Tesla Showroom*
在哥德堡
特斯拉展廳
視察
下一代的汽車

M6236 - Tuesday, August 23, 2016

Dear Martin:

Have arrived Oslo from Göteborg via Karlstad 2 days ago, and after looking out of my humble hotel room window in the morning, could not believe my neighbor is Oslo Grand Hotel (opened at the same time and same name as the Stockholm one which is famous for accommodating Nobel prize winners), as well as the Royal Palace (at the end of the boulevard), as shown in the photo #A1!

2 天前兩天前從哥德堡經卡爾斯塔德抵達奧斯陸後，早上從我很普通的酒店房間的窗戶往外看後，簡直不敢相信我的鄰居是奧斯陸大酒店（與斯德哥爾摩以接待諾貝爾獎獲得者而聞名的同名酒店同時開業），以及皇宮（在林蔭大道的盡頭），如照片#A1 所示！

Moreover, as shown in the photo #A2，during the visit of Oslo Vigeland Museum, I was very surprised to find out the sculpture "The Tree Hugger" outside a 2012 Norman Foster building ("The Bow") very similar to one of Gustav Vigeland's bronze statues!

此外，如照片#A2 所示，在參觀奧斯陸維格蘭博物館期間，我非常驚訝地發現諾曼福斯特於 2012 年完成的其中一間大樓（"弓河"）外的雕塑"抱樹者"與古斯塔夫維格蘭的青銅雕像非常相似！

Meanwhile, after visiting many museums and talking to the guide in Oslo, and as shown in the photo #A3，I believe Norwegians still have the seafaring adventurous spirit of Viking (the tour guide told me most of the Norwegians *owned a boat), and they are very proud of this period of history!*

　　同時，在參觀了奧斯陸的許多博物館並與導遊交談後，而如照片#A3所示，我相信挪威人仍然具有維京人的航海冒險精神(導遊告訴我大部分挪威人都有自己的船)，他們並對這段歷史時期感到非常自豪！

M6236 - A1
(DSC03898)
Oslo Grand Hotel
奧斯陸大酒店

M6236 - A2
(DSC03565)
Bronze Statue at
Oslo Vigeland Museum
奧斯陸維格蘭博物館
的青銅雕像

M6236 - A3
(DSC03694)
Sailing at the rough
Oslofjorden
航行在驚濤駭浪的
奧斯陸峽灣

64

3.0 Northern & Central Europe
北歐與中歐

3.2 *Germany, Czechia, Hungary*
德國、捷克、匈牙利

3.2.1 *Hamburg* 漢堡
3.2.2 *Berlin* 柏林
3.2.3 *Praha, Budapest*
布拉格、布達佩斯

3.2.1
Hamburg 漢堡

M4217 - Tuesday, August 5, 2014

Dear Martin:

As shown in photo # A1 - A2, I am very surprised that as a harbour city, Hamburg's downtown canal and Binnenalster are so beautiful!

如照片#A1 - A2 所示， 作為海港城市，我很驚訝漢堡市中心的運河與內阿爾斯特湖是如此美！

As to the photo#A3, the senior management of McDonald in Oak Brook will have heart attack when they know about the exciting location of their "family" restaurant at the world famous Hamburg Reeperbahn!

至於照片#A3，美國奧克布魯克麥當勞總部的高層當知道他們的"家庭"餐廳在世界著名的漢堡繩索街的激動人心的位置時將會心臟病發作！

M4126 - A1
(DSC00361)
Canal at Hamburg Downtown
漢堡市中心運河

M4126 - A2
Hamburg
City Centre
Binnenalster
漢堡市中心
之
內阿爾斯特湖

(DSC00381)

(DSC00367)

M4126 - A3
(DSC00331a)
McDonald at
Hamburg
Reeperbahn
漢堡繩索街的
麥當勞

3.2.2
Berlin 柏林

M4220 - Friday, August 8, 2014

Dear Martin:

Have arrived Berlin from Hamburg two days ago, and was surprised my hotel is a new building - until I find out it is located in East Berlin. After more than 20 years of unification, East Berlin is still a "wok-in-progress".

兩天前從漢堡抵達柏林，很奇怪我這家酒店是一座新建築 - 直到我發現它位於東柏林。統一了 **20** 多年之後，東柏林仍是"半成品"。

Meanwhile, as shown in photos #A1 - A3, I have visited Checkpoint Charlie, Cold War Museum, and Berlin Wall today, and found this experience quite shocking!

與此同時，如照片**#A1 -A3** 所示，我今天去了查理檢查站、冷戰博物館、及柏林围墙，覺得這次經歷相當震撼！

M4220 - A1
(DSC00589)
At Berlin Checkpoint Charlie
在柏林查理檢查站

M4220 - A2
(DSC00594)
At Berlin
Cold War
Museum
在柏林
冷戰博物館

M4220 - A3
At East / West
Sides
of Berlin Wall
在柏林圍牆的
東/西方

(DSC00573)

(DSC00570)

3.2.3
Praha, Budapest
布拉格、布達佩斯

M4225 - Wednesday, August 13, 2014

Dear Martin:

After spending few days in Praha, I am now in Budapest and very surprised to find this city, besides having a lower cost of living, English is almost the second language (her famous Chain Bridge, is designed by English and constructed by Scots)!

在布拉格停留了幾天后，我已到了布達佩斯，並很驚訝地發現這座城市除了生活費用較低之外，英語幾乎是第二語言（其著名的鏈橋是由英格蘭人設計並由蘇格蘭人建造）！

Moreover, thanks for your 2 e-mails! The hotel you have stayed at the Pest I believe should be the red circled InterContinental in the photo #A1 - excellent view of the Danube and the Palace!

此外，感謝您來的 2 封電子郵件！你曾住在佩斯的酒店我相信應該是照片#A1 中紅圈的那間洲際酒店 - 絕佳位置去觀看多瑙河和皇宮的美景！

As to Photo #A2, the Best Western building in Praha, built in 1307, is 10-15 minutes walk from central train station, and right in the theatre district. First night I have Carmen opera/ballet in Theatre Hybernia, and another evening the Bohemian Symphony Orchestra Praha performance (Hollywood Movie Music!) at Smetana Hall (former Royal Court palace), all within 5 minutes walk from hotel!

至於照片#A2, 這是布拉格的最佳西方酒店大樓, 建
於 1307 年, 距離中央火車站步行約 10-15 分鐘, 并位於劇
院區。第一天晚上, 我在海伯尼亞劇院觀看了卡門芭蕾舞/
歌劇, 另一晚則在斯美塔那演奏廳（前皇家宮殿）聆聽了
布拉格波西米亞交響樂團的表演 (演奏好萊塢電影音樂!),
這兩處距離我住的酒店都只有 5 分鐘的步行路程!

M4225 - A1
(DSC01268a)
InterContinental
in Pest
佩斯洲際酒店

M4225 - A2
(DSC01052)
Best Western Praha
in
Old Town Praha
布拉格老城裡
最佳西方
布拉格酒店

4.0 Eastern Europe 東歐

4.1 *Russia* 俄羅斯

4.1.1 *Moskva* 莫斯科

M4247 -Thursday, September 4, 2014

Dear Martin:

Have arrived Moscow from Shanghai yesterday evening, and found the public transport (express train + metro) from the airport to the hotel very convenient. Due to Russian visa required invitation letter, so have to stay at a "respectable" host like 5-star hotel!

昨天晚上從上海到達了莫斯科，並發覺現從機場到酒店的公共交通工具（快車 +地鐵）非常方便。由於俄羅斯簽證需要邀請函，因此住在五星級酒店等"高尚的"接待單位比較好！

As to photos #A1 - A2， I am most impressed by the Moscow Red Square GUM department store, beautifully built in 1890!

至於照片#A1 - A2， 莫斯科紅場裡的古姆國家百貨商場給我留下了極深刻的印象，該美麗的商店建於 1890 年！

M4247 - A1
(DSC03442)
Beautiful
Red Square GUM
Department Store
美麗的紅場
古姆國家百貨商場

M4247 - A2
(DSC03452)
Very Modern
GUM
Department
Store
現代感很強的
古姆
國家百貨商場

M4247 - A3
(DSC03605)
Morning at Red
Square
紅場早上

M4247 - A4
(DSC03598)
From Russia
With Love
俄羅斯之戀

4.0 Eastern Europe 東歐

4.2 *Bulgaria, Romania, Ukraine, Poland*
保加利亞、羅馬尼亞 烏克蘭、波蘭

4.2.1 *Sofija* 索非亞
4.2.2 *București* 布加勒斯特
4.2.3 *Kyiv*基輔
4.2.4 *Warszawa* 華沙

4.2.1
Sofija 索非亞

Dear Martin:

Have arrived Sofija from Gatwick last Monday, and find Bulgaria has just awoken from the communist economy (even though the democratically elected government has been in place since 1989), so cost of living very low (as shown in photos #A1 - A2).

上週一從倫敦蓋特威克機場到達索非亞，發現保加利亞還是剛剛從共產主義經濟中醒來（即使自 **1989** 年以來，民主選舉產生的政府就已經到位），因此生活成本很低（如照片**#A1-A2** 所示）。

Meanwhile, as shown in photos #A3, I have good time in Sofija, and I find her 4,000+ years history fascinating - Roman emperor Constantine spent most of his reign in this city as he was born not far from here!

同時，如照片**#A3** 所示，我在索非亞度過了愉快的時光，並發現她 **4,000** 多年以上的歷史非常迷人 - 羅馬皇帝君士坦丁在這個城市中度過了大部分統治帝國的時間，因為他是在離這裡不遠的地方出生！

M8135 - A1
(DSC02261)
Sofija very modern
German Kaufland
supermarket
索非亞非常現代化的
德國考夫蘭超市

M8135 - A2
(DSC02275)
Buguettes at
Kaufland supermarket
cost
USD 20 cents each
考夫蘭超市的
法式長棍麵包
每個花費 **20** 美分

M8135 - A3
Enjoying Bulgarian
Wine and Sausages
享受保加利亞的
葡萄酒和香腸

DSC02169

DSC02167

79

<u>M8141 - Monday, May 21, 2018</u>
(*This eMail sent from Kyiv Boryspil International Airport*)
(這電郵從基輔鮑里斯波爾國際機場發出)

Dear Martin:

Have arrived Bucureşti from Sofia on May 18, 2018 via twin propeller engine plane. It is only about one hour (220 miles) but fully seated, while my flight from Bucureşti to Kyiv (also jam-packed) has to go through Paris CDG airport! This shows among the Balkan states, they are not too excited to cross each other's land border, even though most of them are EU members.

2018 年 5 月 18 日乘雙螺旋槳發動機飛機從索非亞到達了布加勒斯特。它只飛行約一個小時（220 英里），但全滿，而我從布加勒斯特到基輔的航班（也被擠滿了），需要回頭經過巴黎戴高樂機場！這表明在巴爾幹半島的國家，即使他們大部分都是歐盟成員，也並不會很願意讓對方輕易跨越陸路邊界。

Moreover, as shown in photo #A1, very excited to see the Black Sea and the end of River Danube from the 2 ½ hours (one way) train ride to Constanţa. I am especially moved by the vending machine at the Bucureşti main railway station (i.e., Gare du Nord – Latin is the official language of România) containing not soda but books with title like <u>I-Ching</u> (as shown in red circle of photo)!

同時，如照片#A1 所示，在乘坐 2½小時（單程）的火車前往康斯坦察時很高興看到多瑙河的末端和黑海。我特別受到布加勒斯特火車總站（即北站 **Gare du nord -** 拉

80

丁語是羅馬尼亞的官方語言）的自動售貨機所感動，因為這裡售賣的不是飲料，而是中國的<u>易經</u>和其他書籍（如照片#A2紅圈所示）！

M8141 - A1 (DSC02608)
View of Black Sea from Constanţa IBIS Hotel
從康斯坦察宜必思酒店欣賞黑海美景

M8141 - A2 (DSC02480)
Vending machine selling I-Ching and other books
at Bucureşti Gare du Nord
在布加勒斯特北站
提供易經的書籍售貨機

4.2.3
Kyiv 基輔

M8144 - Thursday, May 24, 2018

Dear Martin:

 Have arrived Kyiv on May 22, 2018, and have found this city is quite cosmopolitan, you feel like you are in any of the large cities in Western Europe, but real estate price is cheap (as shown in photo #A1), and the cost of living is very low - the tour guide said thanks for not using Euro!

 2018 年 5 月 22 日抵達基輔，發現這個城市非常國際化，感覺就像置身於西歐任何一個大城市，但房地產價格便宜 (如照片#A1 所示)，生活成本也很低 —— 嚮導說這是由於他們不用歐元所致！

 Meanwhile, as shown in as shown in photo #A3 - A4, have good time in Kyiv, and the whole city has great festive mood for the May 26 Liverpool vs Real Madrid Champions League Final. And during breakfast at the hotel this morning, the occupants of all the tables close to me were speaking English very much like Beatles!

 同時，如照片#A2 - A3 所示，在基輔度過了愉快的時光，整個城市都為 5 月 26 日利物浦對皇家馬德里的冠軍聯賽決賽而歡呼雀躍。今天早上在酒店吃早餐時，所有靠近我的桌子上的客人都說著非常像披頭士樂隊口音的英語！

M8144 - A1
(DSC02805)
New apartment costs USD 35 per sq. ft
新公寓
每平方英尺
35 美元

M8144 - A2
(DSC02733)
Overview of Kyiv Old Town & Dnipro River
基輔老城和
第聶伯河概覽

M8144 - A3
Promotion at Kyiv for May 26 Liverpool vs Real Madrid Champions League Final
在基輔舉行的
5 月 26 日利物浦對
皇家馬德里
冠軍決賽
的推廣活動

(DSC02978)

M8144 - Monday, May 28, 2018

Dear Martin:

Have arrived Warszawa from Kyiv by air (again jam-packed) on May 25, 2018, and was very surprised that there were only 2 persons (I was the first one) went through the "All Passport" (i.e., non-EU) counter. There was about half planeload of "Non-Schengen" transfer, and I suspect they are Russians visiting their relatives in Ukraine, as the flights from Kyiv to Moscow have been stopped.

2018 年 5 月 25 日從基輔乘飛機（再次非常擁擠）抵達華沙，非常驚訝只有 2 人（我是第一個）通過了 "所有護照類"（即非歐盟公民）櫃檯，而 "非申根協定" 中轉的佔這班飛機乘客總數大約一半，我懷疑他們是俄羅斯人在烏克蘭探親，因為從基輔到莫斯科的航班已經停止飛行。

Meanwhile, as shown in photo #A1 - A2, have good time in Warszawa, even though the city is still recovering from the ruins of 90% damage at the end of 2nd World War!

同時，如照片 #A1 - A2 所示，我在華沙度過很愉快的時光 ——儘管這座城市仍在從第二次世界大戰結束時 90% 損壞的廢墟中恢復過來！

M8148 - A1 (DSC03224)
At Warszawa Old Town Castle Square
(All buildings in this photo rebuilt from ruins after WWII)
攝於華沙老城城堡廣場
（這照片裡的所有建築物 都是二戰後從廢墟中重建的）

M8144 - A2 (DSC03241)
Enjoying coffee and Polish donut with famous people
at Warszawa Old Town Castle Square
在華沙老城城堡廣場
與名人一起享用咖啡和波蘭甜甜圈

5.0 Southern Europe 南歐

5.1 *Italy* 意大利

5.1.1 *Genova* 熱那亞
5.1.2 *Milano* 米蘭
5.1.3 *Napoli* 那不勒斯

M5274 - Thursday, October 1, 2015

Dear Martin:

Have spent few days at Nice, very impressed about the upper and lower corniche to Monte Carlo（sitting next to the driver of the minibus), and arrived Genova yesterday by train. After checking in the hotel, walked to the Porto Antico, and found the quayside in the evening was pretty rough, quite similar to the Vieux-Port of Marseill!. However, in the daytime, it is a lot of fun to visit, like the shop selling old camera, as shown in photos #A1.

在尼斯停留了幾天，對來回蒙特卡洛的上下濱海路印象深刻（我坐在旅遊小巴司機旁邊），昨天乘火車到了熱那亞。入住酒店後，步行前往古港，發現碼頭傍晚時江湖人士不少，與馬賽的舊港很相像！不過白天逛倒是很有趣的，比如看看賣舊相機的店，如照片**#A1**所示。

In any case, never imagine my trip to Genova will be a cultural one - visited 4 museums today! 3 of them covered by 48 hours Museum Card, allowing you to visit 21 museums, which is a great deal for €16! The 4th one I had to pay another €11 (after Museum card discount) viewing Monet, Renoir, Degas, Cezanne, Van Gogh, Matisse, Picasso..., and these paintings all came from Detroit Institute of Arts (DIA) for short term exhibition. I suspect this tour may be one of the ways to help paying for the 800 million dollars demanded by the city to let DIA to be owned by citizen group!

無論如何，永遠想像不到我的熱那亞之行會是一場文化之旅 — 今天參觀了 **4** 家博物館！其中 **3** 間不另收費包含在博物館卡（此卡花 **16** 歐元於 **48** 小時內可以參觀 **21** 家博物館！）。第 4 間博物館我需要另外支付 11 歐元（在博物館卡折扣之後）觀看莫奈、雷諾阿、德加、塞尚、梵高、馬蒂斯、畢加索……的畫，而這些短期展覽的名畫均來自美國底特律藝術博物館（**DIA**）。我懷疑這次名畫展覽國際之旅可能是民間團體用來幫助支付給該市出讓 **DIA** 所要求的 **8** 億美元的籌款活動之一！

Meanwhile, very happy to have great pizza in the quayside pizzeria last night, and excellent pasta & tiramisu this evening in a Michelin starred trattoria just opposite from my hotel, as shown in photo #A2!

同時，很高興昨晚在碼頭邊的比薩餅餐館吃了很棒的披薩，今晚在我酒店對面的一家米其林星級餐廳吃了出色的意大利面和提拉米蘇, 如照片#A2 所示！

M5724 - A1
(DSC08562)
*Genova Quayside
Used Camera Store*
熱那亞碼頭
二手相機店

M5724 - A2
(DSC08744)
*Tiramisu at
Genova Trattoria
'Al Veliero'*
熱那亞
"致帆船"餐廳的
提拉米蘇

5.1.2
Milano 米蘭

M5277 - Sunday, October 4, 2015

Dear Martin:

Have arrived Milan from Genova two days ago by train, and visited Milan Expo 2015 yesterday, with food as its theme. Even though the size of this Expo is much smaller than Shanghai 2010, however, I find the atmosphere is very exciting - seems like a big party! Every visitor is eating and eating and eating, encouraged by the theme of the participated countries, as shown in photos #A1!

兩天前從熱那亞坐火車到米蘭，昨天去了 2015 年米蘭世博會，以美食為主題。雖然這次世博會的規模比 2010 年上海世博會小很多，但是我覺得氣氛很熱鬧 ── 好像是個大派對！每一位參觀者都被參展國家的主題所鼓舞，吃、吃、吃、吃，如照片 **#A1** 所示！

After experiencing Milan's shopping craziness at the Duomo, I have a very pleasant day at the Lake Como by the Swiss border. From Milan's Porta Garibaldi train station (about 5 minutes' walk from my hotel), I took a local train to Como, and got off at the wrong station - one stop earlier. Luckily, the train driver suspected correctly that this Asian tourist's destination should be the next station (I was the only one got off at this tiny stop), watching me enquiring the platform workers, the whole train waited for 5 minutes, then opened the door to allow me re-board! Thus, as you can see from photos #A2, starting from Como and ending at Lecco, the ferry stops over 15 ports of call, I find these small villages, comparing with Milan, almost like living in another world!

90

在米蘭大教堂廣場體驗了可以瘋狂購物之後，我在瑞士邊境的科莫湖度過了非常愉快的一天。從米蘭的加里波第門火車站（距離我的酒店步行約5分鐘），我乘坐短途火車前往科莫，在錯誤的車站（提前了一站）下車。幸運的是，列車駕駛員猜對了這位亞洲人遊客的目的地應該是下一站(我是這小站下車的唯一乘客)，看著我詢問站台工作人員，整個列車等了5分鐘，然後開車門給我重新上車！因此，從照片#A2可以看出，從科莫到萊科，渡輪停靠了超過15個站口，我發現這些小村莊，和米蘭相比，簡直就像是生活在另一個世界！

M5277 - A1
(DSC08863
Milan Expo
Italy Theme
"Eataly"
米蘭世博會
意大利館主題
"吃在意大利"

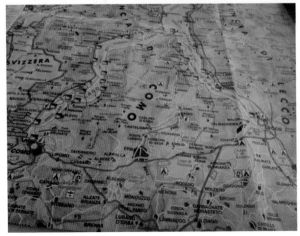

M5277 - A2
(DSC09203)
Lake Como
Ferry
Stops 15+
Ports of Call
渡輪停靠
超過15個
科莫湖站口

5.1.3
Napoli 那不勒斯

M5274 - Thursday, October 1, 2015

Dear Martin:

Have arrived Napoli from Milano 2 days ago, and have tried pizzeria with no seats, with no tablecloth (Da Michele - Michelin starred, as shown in photo # A1), and with tablecloth (Brandi - the inventor of Margherita Pizza), I find the taste of all three were good, as the pizza was delivered to me sitting (or standing) only several feet from the oven!

兩天前從米蘭到那不勒斯，我嘗試了沒有座位（站著吃的比薩店）、沒有桌布（達米歇爾店-米其林星級餐廳）、和有桌布（布蘭迪店-瑪格麗特披薩的發明者）。我發現這三種食法的味道都很好，因為無論是坐著（或站著）等披薩，我離開烤箱都只有幾英尺的距離！

Moreover, as shown in photo # A2, have found the Napoli sfogliatella very delicious, and surprised why I never heard of it!

再者，如照片#A2所示，我發現那不勒斯千層酥非常好吃，並很奇怪為什麼我從來沒有聽說過這個好東西！

Meanwhile, as shown in photos # A3-A4, I have found the cleanliness of Capri and Sorrento is no different from the French Riviera, which indicates that Italian can be as good as the French!

同時，如照片#A3-A4所示，我發現卡普里島和索倫托鎮的清潔程度與法國里維埃拉沒有什麼不同，這表明意大利人可以幹的和法國人一樣好！

92

M5790 – A1
(DSC09448)
Enjoy Da Michele Pizza
next to the oven
在烤箱旁享用
達米歇爾披薩

M5790 – A2
(DSC09426)
Afternoon Coffee with
Napoli Sfogliatella
享用下午茶之咖啡與
那不勒斯千層酥

M5790 - A3
(DSC09625)
Happy Tourist at
Capri's Faraglioni
在卡普里島奇岩
的快樂遊客

M5790 - A4 (DSC09314 & DSC09348)
Sorrento Excelsior Vittoria & Town Centre
索倫托怡東维多利亞酒店與镇中心

93

5.0 Southern Europe 南歐

5.2 *Greece, Türkiye*
希臘、土耳其

5.2.1 *Athína* 雅典
5.2.2 *Istanbul* 伊斯坦布爾

Athína 雅典

<u>M5287 - Wednesday, October 14, 2015</u>

Dear Martin:

Have arrived Athína from Roma 5 days ago, and have good feeling about Greece. I find Greeks are quite "Spartan" in their personal spending, such as their popular €0.50 Koulouri breakfast, as shown in photo #A1. Athína's streets are also very clean, and as shown in photo #A2, they really love marble!

5 天前從羅馬抵達雅典，對希臘很有好感。我發現希臘人在個人消費方面相當 "斯巴達式" 節儉，比如他們很受歡迎的 0.50 歐元的庫盧裡早餐，如圖#A1 所示。雅典的街道也很乾淨，而且如照片#A2 所示，他們非常愛好大理石！

Visited the Temple of Apollo on the next day, learning the Greek myths along the way. On arriving Delphi, the rain poured so hard that we were unable to visit the site, and had to take quite a long walk to the museum. I asked the learned guide (I find the Greek tour guides are very professional with immense knowledge of the destination) which god in charge of the rainfall as I was not happy about this raining situation. It was Zeus (father of Apollo), the first guy from the left in photo #A3. 20 minutes later (we were still in museum), the sun shined brightly - Zeus had spoken!

到的第二天參觀了阿波羅神廟，一路學習希臘神話。到達德爾斐時，傾盆大雨，我們無法先參觀該遺址，不得不步行去挺遠的博物館。我問博學的導遊（我發現希臘導遊非常專業，對目的地有豐富的知識）哪個神負責降雨，因為我對這種下雨的情況很不滿意。導遊告訴我應是

宙斯（阿波羅的父親），即照片#A3左起第一個人。20分
鐘後（我們還在博物館裡），陽光普照 — 宙斯表態了！

*Meanwhile, while in Athína, have learned the origins
of many English words, like panic (from Greek myth "Pan"),
etc., but the most interesting one is the possible incorrect use
of Greek banker's caduceus by the U.S. medical professional
as their icon!*

同時，在雅典期間，了解了很多英文單詞的來源，
像 panic（來自希臘神話"Pan"）等，但最有趣的是希臘
銀行家的雙蛇克丟西爾斯杖可能錯誤地被美國醫學界採用
為他們的圖標！

M5287 - A1 (DSC00379)
*Athenians' €0.50
Koulouri breakfast*
雅典人 0.50 歐元的
庫盧裡早餐

M5287 - A2 (DSC00452)
Athína Marbled Road
雅典大理石路

M5287 - A3 (DSC00349)
*From Left -
Zeus, Niki, & Athena)*
左起 -
宙斯、尼基、
和雅典娜

5.2.2
Istanbul 伊斯坦布爾

M4235 - Saturday, August 23, 2014

Dear Martin:

Have spent few days each at Wien and München, enjoyed the Schweinshaxe Bavarian roast pork knuckle at the tourist spot Hofbräuhaus, as shown in photo #A1, then very excited to arrive Istanbul, as this place everything is Europe/Asia (as shown in photo #A2), and the history dated back to "B.C."! My hotel here is quite nice - complimentary sea view room, complimentary full breakfast, high quality service, right in the old town, and 3 minutes walking to Grand Bazaar!

在維也納和慕尼黑分別逗留了幾天，於遊客勝地皇家啤酒屋享用巴伐利亞烤豬肘，如照片#A1所示，然後非常興奮地來到了伊斯坦布爾，因為這個地方一切都是歐洲/亞洲分界（如照片#A2所示），歷史可以追溯到"公元前"！我住的酒店相當不錯——房間有免費海景、免費全份早餐、優質服務，位置就在老城區，步行3分鐘到大巴扎！

Meanwhile, as shown in photo #A3，have tried the Turkish coffee and found it was quite good - very smooth and not bitter, but unable to tell the fortune from reading the residue in the cup!

同時，如照片#A3所示，嘗試了土耳其咖啡，發現它非常好 - 很順滑，不苦，但不懂如何通過杯子中的殘留物來算命！

M4223 - A1 (DSC02240 & DSC02251)
Enjoyed Hofbräuhaus
Schweinshaxe Bavarian roast pork knuckle
享用慕尼黑皇家啤酒屋巴伐利亞烤豬肘

M4223 - A2
(DSC02953)
View of Europe from Asia
at the popular Galata Tower
在著名的加拉塔塔
從亞洲看到的歐洲

M4223 - A3 (DSC02476)
Fortune telling from reading
Turkish coffee residue
通過閱讀土耳其咖啡渣
來算命

M4223 - A4 (DSC02343)
Very tasty Turkish Baklava
非常好吃的
土耳其巴克拉瓦
果仁蜜浆千層酥

99

6.0 The Mediterranean Islands
地中海島嶼

6.1 *Cyprus* 塞浦路斯
6.2 *Kríti, Santorini* 克里特島、聖托里尼島
6.3 *Malta* 馬耳他
6.4 *Sicily* 西西里
6.5 *Sardegna* 撒丁島
6.6 *Còrsega* 科西嘉島

101

<u>*M7140 - Saturday, May 20, 2017*</u>

Dear Martin:

Have arrived Limassol from Kríti via the very modern Cyprus Larnaca International Airport on May 17, 2017. As Limassol is about 40 miles from the airport, thus, returned today to Larnaca to stay overnight for tomorrow's flight to Malta.

2017 年 5 月 17 日從克里特經過非常現代化的塞浦路斯拉納卡國際機場抵達利馬索爾。由於利馬索爾距離機場約 40 英里，因此今天返回拉納卡過夜，準備明天飛往馬耳他。

In the last 4 days, have visited quite a number of cities on the island, including the Greek Cypriot's Pafos, Limassol, & Larnaca, and Turkish Cypriot's Keryneia (passport required) , plus both sides of the divided Nicosia (its "Checkpoint Charlie" is a major tourist draw!), and have good time in the in both sides of Cyprus, as shown in photos #A1 - A2!

在過去的 4 天裡，去了島上相當多的城市，包括希族塞人的帕福斯、利馬索爾、和拉納卡，和土族塞人的克雷尼亞（需要護照過檢查站），以及分裂的尼科西亞兩側（其類似柏林的 "查理檢查站" 是一個主要的旅遊景點！），在塞浦路斯南北兩邊玩得很開心，如照片 #A1-A2 所示！

Meanwhile, I have found the politics of Cyprus is quite explosive, because: (a) the Greek Cypriot tour guide and tourist maps all called North Cyprus "Area Under Turkish

Occupation Since 1974"; and (b) the taxi driver in Limassol angrily told me that "there is NO North Cyprus (a term used by Turkish Cypriots), but only one Cyprus!"

　　與此同時，我發現塞浦路斯的政治極具爆炸性，因為：**(a)** 希族塞人導遊和旅遊地圖都稱北塞浦路斯為 "自 **1974** 年以來土耳其占領的地區"；與 **(b)** 利馬索爾的出租車司機憤怒地告訴我 "那裡 不是北塞浦路斯（土族塞人使用的術語），因為只有一個塞浦路斯！"

M7140 - A1
(DSC07636)
Fresh orange juice tasted like honey at Keryneia
在克雷尼亞的
鮮榨橙汁
嘗起來像蜂蜜一樣

M7140 - A2
(DSC08744)
With
Ferrai 308 GTS
at Limassol
在利馬索爾與
法拉利 **308 GTS**
合照

Kríti, Santorini

克里特島、聖托里尼島

M7135 - Saturday, May 16, 2017

Dear Martin:

Have arrived Heraklion, the largest city of Kríti, from Athína, in the afternoon of May 13, 2017, amid very hot weather of about 95°F, and taken jet propelled boat to visit Santorini the day after.

2017 年 5 月 13 日下午在天氣非常炎熱（約 95° F）下從雅典抵達克里特島最大城市伊拉克利翁, 然後於第三天乘噴氣推進船去聖托里尼島。

While in Heraklion, besides going to Chania as well, have visited the city's 2 most famous historical landmarks, i.e., Koules Fortress and Knossos Palace. I have been amazed by the first one, i.e., 21-year of siege by the very strong Ottoman forces at this Venetian fortress, as shown in Photo#A1, and confused greatly by the second landmark. It is because as shown in Photo #A2, except the rock foundation from the ruins, the rest of this existing Knossos Palace is cement and re-constructed based on the imagination of Sir Arthur Evans, as discussed in Chapter 7.

除了去干尼亞市之外, 在伊拉克利翁期間, 參觀了該城最著名的 2 個歷史地標, 即庫勒斯要塞和克諾索斯宮。我對第一個感到驚訝, 因為非常強大的奧斯曼軍隊圍攻這座威尼斯人控制的堡壘長達 21 年之久。對第二個地標則感到非常困惑。這是因為如圖#A2 所示, 除了廢墟的岩石基礎外, 現有的克諾索斯宮殿的其餘部分都是水泥, 是亞瑟・埃文斯爵士根據他的想像而重建的, 如第 7 章所討論的。

M7135 - A1
(DSC07116)
Heraklion
Koules Fortress
伊拉克利翁
庫勒斯要塞

M7135 - A2
(DSC06653)
Heraklion
Knossos Palace
伊拉克利翁
克諾索斯宮

M7135 - A3
(DSC06930)
Afternoon
coffee and cake
at Oia's cafe
在伊亞鎮咖啡館
享受下午茶
咖啡與蛋糕

M7143 - Monday, May 22, 2017

Dear Martin:

Have arrived Malta from Cyprus on May 21, 2017 afternoon, via the very fancy Emirates Airline, i.e., state-of-the-art Boeing 777-300, comfortable seats, "live" sports programs, and excellent meal - but no Coca-Cola or Pepsi!

乘坐非常豪華的阿聯酋航空公司，有最先進的波音 777-300、舒適的座椅、"現場"體育節目、和美味的餐點 —— 但沒有可口可樂或 百事可樂供應, 於 2017 年 5 月 21 日下午從塞浦路斯抵達馬耳他!

Moreover, even though I have visited many European harbours, however, as shown in photos #A1 to #A3, Malta's armed-to-the-teeth (both German & Italian navies did not dare to try a frontal attack of the Valletta castles during the whole period of World War II) Grand and Marsamxetto harbours are really an eye-opener and the view is breathtaking!

此外，儘管我去過許多歐洲港口，但是，如照片#A1 到#A2 所示，馬耳他全副武裝到牙齒的大港和馬薩姆西託港（整個二戰期間, 德國和意大利海軍都不敢嘗試正面攻擊瓦萊塔市的城堡）真是大開眼界，景色令人嘆為觀止!

M7143 - A1
(DSC07986)
*Hearty
hotel breakfast
with a view*
豐盛的
酒店早餐
和美景

(DSC08095)

M7143 - A2
*Valletta's
Grand Harbour*
瓦萊塔的大港

(DSC08345)

Sicily 西西里

M7149 - Monday, May 29, 2017

Dear Martin:

Referring to your e-mail, as Taormina has been sealed off tightly, i.e., no outsiders, since I have arrived Sicily (Catania) from Malta on May 23, 2017, hence, I have no chance to say hello to President Trump, and as shown in the photo #A1, it seems the Sicilians are not too excited about the G7 Summit!

有關你來的郵件，由於在 2017 年 5 月 23 日從馬耳他抵達西西里島（卡塔尼亞）以來，陶爾米納一直被嚴密封鎖，不許外人進入，因此，我沒有機會與特朗普總統打招呼，并如照片 #A1 所示，西西里人似乎對 G7 峰會不感到太興奮！

Moreover, have arrived Palermo yesterday (May 28, 2017) early afternoon by train, and as shown in photos #A2 - A4, have good time in Sicily, and will fly to Cagliari of Sardegna tomorrow!

此外，已於昨天（2017 年 5 月 28 日）下午早些時候乘火車抵達巴勒莫，並如照片#A2 - #A4 所示，在西西里玩的很開心，明天就飛撒丁島的卡利亞里！

M7149 - A1
(DSC09357)
Palermo Poster
Against G7
反對 **G7** 的巴勒莫海報

M7149 - A2
(DSC09081)
Quite tasty
Sicilian Baked Rice
With Ham & Cheese
很好吃的
西西里
火腿芝士焗飯

M7149 - A3
(DSC08773)
At Mt. Etna
Summit Crater
攝於
埃特纳
顶峰火山口

M7149 - A4
(DSC09199)
Crossing
Strait of Messina
to Mainland Italy
從西西里
横渡墨西拿海峡
到意大利大陸

109

6.5
Sardegna 撒丁島

M7152 - Thursday, June 1, 2017

Dear Martin:

Have arrived Cagliari from Palermo on May 30, 2017 and experienced 3 surprises: (1) From airport costing me only €1.30 and about 5 minutes high speed train to downtown, and this is the first surprise; (2) The second surprise of Sardegna island is its capital Cagliari is very clean, as shown in photos #A1; and (3) The third surprise is a rare one, i.e., while travelling northward 180 miles across Sardegna on high speed train, as shown in photos #A2, besides costing me only €18, there is no appearance of ticket inspector for entire trip!

2017 年 5 月 30 日從巴勒莫抵達卡利亞里並經歷了 3 次驚喜：（1）從機場僅花費 1.30 歐元和大約 5 分鐘的高速火車到市中心，這是第一個驚喜; (2) 撒丁島的第二個驚喜是它的首都卡利亞里非常乾淨，如圖#A1 所示; (3) 第三個驚喜是難得一見的，即當乘坐高速列車向北行駛 180 英里穿過撒丁島，如圖 #A2 所示，除了只花了我 18 歐元之外，全程沒有檢票員出現！

Meanwhile, as shown in photos #A3, will take ferry from Sardegna to Còrsega this afternoon!

另一個方面，如圖 #A3 所示，我今天下午將乘渡輪從撒丁島前往科西嘉島！

ML7152 - A1
(DSC09490)
**Downtown
Cagliari**
卡利亞里市中心

M7152 - A2
(DSC09559)
*Cross Sardegna
High Speed Train*
穿越撒丁島的
高速列車

M7149 - A3
(DSC09605)
*Ferry from
Sardegna
to Còrsega*
從撒丁島到
科西嘉島的渡輪

Còrsega 科西嘉島

Dear Martin:

Have arrived Còrsega from Sardegna by ferry on June 1, 2017, and are very impressed by the cliffs of the Castle of Bonifacio, as shown in photos #A1.

2017 年 6 月 1 日從撒丁島乘渡輪抵達科西嘉島，並對博尼法喬城堡的懸崖印象深刻，如照片#A1 所示。

As to the hometown of Napoleon, i.e., Ajaccio, everywhere is about her favorite son. Besides the airport called Napoleon Bonaparte, and the Maison Bonaparte (Napoleon's birth place and home until he went to mainland France) becomes national museum, there are many statues of Napoleon, even in the place where General de Gaulle announced his return to France on October 8, 1943, as shown in photos #A2!

至於拿破崙的故鄉阿雅克修，處處都是關於她最寵愛的兒子。除了名為拿破崙・波拿巴的機場，以及成為國家博物館的波拿巴之家（拿破崙的出生地和他去法國大陸之前的家）之外，還有許多拿破崙的雕像，甚至也出現在戴高樂將軍於 1943 年 10 月 8 日宣布返回法國的地方，如照片 #A2 所示！

Meanwhile, have good time in Còrsega, and will take the Civitavecchia ferry tomorrow to Italy mainland, staying 3 nights in Roma before returning home!

同時，在科西嘉玩的很開心，明天坐奇維塔韋基亞渡輪去意大利本土，在羅馬住 3 晚後回國！

M7155 - A1
(DSC09709 &
DSC0987)
Crossing the
Strait of Bonifacio
to arrive Còrsega
from Sardegna
從撒丁島
穿過博尼法喬海峽
到達科西嘉島

M7152 - A4 (DSC00059)
In front of the Statue of Napoleon at
Ajaccio La place du Général-de-Gaulle
攝於阿雅克修戴高樂將軍廣場拿破崙雕像前

7.0 Starting From Knossos
從克諾索斯開始

Reconstruction versus Conservation
論古蹟應該重建或只是養護

2019-10-08

(I) Introduction (引言)

Returning to Heraklion city center on the Route #2 bus from Knossos archaeological site two years ago, I was very much confused by my experience in the previous two hours, and could not help thinking: "Is extensive pouring of concrete onto Knossos by Sir Arthur Evans the right way to restore an archaeological site?"

　　兩年前從克諾索斯考古遺址乘坐 2 路公交車回到伊拉克利翁市中心，我對過去兩個小時的經歷感到非常困惑，不禁想：「阿瑟·埃文斯爵士在克諾索斯大面積澆築混凝土是否為修復古蹟遺址的正確方法嗎？」

Moreover, I have noticed that in A World History of Architecture, full-page color photo of Evans' North Entrance of the Palace of Knossos was posted as the leading picture of Chapter 2, "The Greek World",[1] indicating that it is a very important archaeological site. Thus, in no less confusion than my above mentioned experience at Knossos archaeological site, how come in A History of Architecture: Settings and Rituals, Spiro Kostof (who was Professor of Architectural History at the University of California at Berkeley) used only one sentence "Beginning with the spectacular digging up of Knossos by Sir Arthur Evans"[2] to describe about Evans' entire 30 plus years of extensive linguistic and archaeological contribution to Knossos?

　　此外，我注意到在《世界建築史》書中，埃文斯的克諾索斯宮北門整版彩色照片作為第二章"希臘世界"的主圖被貼上來，表明它是一個非常重要的考古遺址。因此，與我在克諾索斯考古遺址的上述經歷一樣令人困惑的是，在《建築史：設置和儀式》書中，**Spiro Kostof**（曾是加州大學伯克利分校的建築史教授）為什麼只使用了一句子"從阿瑟·埃文斯爵士對克諾索斯的壯觀挖掘開始"來描述埃文斯整整 **30** 多年對克諾索斯的廣泛古語言和考古貢獻？

Hence, the objective of this paper is to find the answer for my above confusions through the following three sources:

因此，本文的目的是通過以下三個來源的文章為我的上述困惑找到答案：

The first article, "The Palace at Knossos (Crete)" by Senta German (who is currently at the Oxford University Ashmolean Museum), presents a balanced viewpoint of the pros and cons of Evans' reconstruction of Knossos. [3]

第一來源的文章是 **Senta German**（目前在牛津大學阿什莫林博物館工作）所寫的 "克諾索斯的宮殿(克里特島)"，對埃文斯重建克諾索斯的利弊提出了平衡的觀點。

The second article, "The introduction to Knossos and the Prophets of Modernism", by Cathy Gere (who is associate professor of history at the University of California at San Diego), is pro-reconstruction, as the author was excited about the "modernist Knossos" and the "concrete Knossos", calling it "one of the first reinforced concrete buildings ever erected on the island". [4]

第二來源的文章是 **Cathy Gere**（加州大學聖地亞哥分校歷史系副教授）所寫的 "克諾索斯簡介和現代主義先知"，是支持重建的，因為作者對 "現代主義之克諾索斯" 和 "混凝土克諾索斯" 感到興奮，稱其為 "島上最早建造的鋼筋混凝土建築之一"。

The third article, "Knossos" by New World Encyclopedia contributors, is against Evans' reconstruction of Knossos. It is because even with no "blueprint of any kind", Evans still proceeded with the extensive pouring of concrete onto this important archaeological site. [5]

第三來源的文章是《新世界百科全書》撰稿人所寫的《克諾索斯》，他們反對埃文斯重建克諾索斯。這是因為即使沒有"任何類型的藍圖"，埃文斯仍然繼續在這個重要的考古遺址上大量澆築混凝土。

(II) Description of Knossos (克諾索斯的描述)

According to Homer's Odyssey, Cnosus (Knossos in Latin) was a great city, ruled by the very wise King Minos, who had the ear of the great Zeus. Under King Minos, around 2000 BCE, his people and the Minoan civilization of Crete flourished. The Athenian architect Daedelus was hired by King Minos to build him a palace protected by the labyrinth, as shown in Exhibit 1. The Knossos Palace was later destroyed two times by fire, around 1700 BCE and 1300 BCE.[6]

根據荷馬的奧德賽，*Cnosus*（拉丁語中的克諾索斯）是一座偉大的城市，由非常睿智的國王米諾斯統治，他得到偉大的宙斯的信任。大約在公元前**2000**年，在米諾斯國王的統治下，他的人民與克里特島的米諾斯文明蓬勃發展。雅典建築師代德羅斯被米諾斯國王聘用，為他建造一座由迷宮保護的宮殿，如圖表**1**所示。克諾索斯宮殿後來兩次被大火燒毀，分別發生在公元前**1700**年和公元前**1300**年左右。

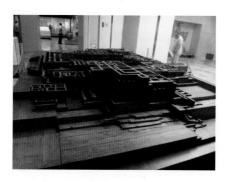

1. Knossos Palace Model at Heraklion Archaeological Museum
伊拉克利翁考古博物馆的克諾索斯宮殿模型

In 1878, a Cretan discovered the destroyed Knossos. However, it was Evans, the British archaeologist, after purchasing the entire site in 1900, started the large-scale excavation.[7] He then reconstructed the Knossos Palace extensively with reinforced concrete, as shown in Exhibits 2 and 3, and.

1878 年，一個克里特島人發現了被毀壞的克諾索斯宮。然而，要到英國考古學家埃文斯在 1900 年購買了整個遺址後，才開始了大規模的挖掘工作。然後，他用鋼筋混凝土對克諾索斯宮進行了大規模重建，如圖表 2 和 3 以及本章扉頁所示。

2. "Concrete Knossos" Example #1
"混凝土的克諾索斯宮" 示例 #1

3. "Concrete Knossos" Example #2
"混凝土的克諾索斯宮" 示例 #2

(III) *Reconstruction Versus Conservation*
論古蹟應該重建或只是養護

In *"The Palace at Knossos (Crete)"*, German felt
Evans' reconstruction helped to uncover very much of
Knossos, and through the architecture and wall paintings
evoked the Minoan civilization.[8] However, she also felt
Evans' reconstruction had not *"accurately reflected what was
found"*[9], and the extensive use of reinforced concrete on
Knossos was against the most important role of restoration, i.e.,
"restorations must be non-destructive and reversible"[10].

在 " 克諾索斯宮殿（克里特島）" 文中，**German**
認為埃文斯的重建有助於揭開克諾索斯的大部分面貌，並
通過建築和壁畫喚起米諾斯文明。然而，她也認為埃文斯
的重建並沒有 " 準確反映發現了什麼 "，而在克諾索斯宮
上廣泛使用鋼筋混凝土違背了修復的最重要作用，即 " 修
復必須是非破壞性和可逆的 " 。

In *"The introduction to Knossos and the Prophets of
Modernism"*, Gere admitted that Evans' reconstruction and
interpretations of Knossos is *"a profoundly ambiguous
bequest"*, the relationship between the forms of the *"modern
fabric"* of Knossos from Evans' reconstruction and the shape
of Bronze Age building was *"far from resolved"*, and *"the
paper reconstruction of the palace in watercolor, pen and ink,
and text, do not easily allow a perspective on the problem
uncolored by the prejudices of Evans and his team"*.[11]

在《克諾索斯與現代主義先知導論》文中，**Gere** 承
認埃文斯對克諾索斯的重建和詮釋是 " 一份極其模糊的遺
贈 "，埃文斯重建的克諾索斯 " 現代結構 " 的形式與現代
主義的關係。青銅時代建築的形狀 " 遠未解決 "，" 用水
彩、筆墨和文字對宮殿進行紙質重建，不容易讓人們對這
個問題產生一種沒有被埃文斯及其團隊的偏見所掩蓋的看
法 " 。

However, in the same paragraph, Gere argued that we should not be "in pursuit of the limestone and gypsum temples built by the people of the Bronze Age". Instead, we should understand the "modernist way with modernist materials" that Evans reconstructed the temple from the perspective of "the age of concrete - the archaeologists, architects, artists, classicists, writers, and poets age of the twentieth century A.D.".[12] She even said parts of Knossos were "pure modernism", looked like "a flimsy Le Corbusier exercise", or "similar to Alexei Shchusev's Lenin Mausoleum in Moscow".[13]

然而，在同一段中，**Gere** 認為我們不應該 "追求青銅時代人們建造的石灰石和石膏廟宇"。相反，我們應該從 "混凝土時代——公元二十世紀的考古學家、建築師、藝術家、古典主義者、作家和詩人的時代" 的角度來理解埃文斯重建神廟的 "現代主義方式與現代主義材料"。她甚至說克諾索斯的部分建築是 "純粹的現代主義"，看起來像是 "脆弱的勒·柯布西耶作品"，或者 "類似於莫斯科的阿列克海·舒謝夫的列寧陵墓"。

In "Knossos", the contributors of the New World Encyclopedia had cast serious doubts on Evans' reconstruction of Knossos as "without blueprints of any kind", he "re-built structures by speculating on how they should have looked". They questioned whether the structure Evans claimed to be King Minos' labyrinth had ever existed. In other words, the reconstructed buildings "appeared authentic", but did not "accurately represent the original Knossos".[14]

在《克諾索斯》文中，《新世界百科全書》的撰稿人對埃文斯重建克諾索斯提出了嚴重質疑，認為他 "沒有任何藍圖"，"通過推測它們應該是什麼樣子來重建結構"。他們質疑埃文斯聲稱是米諾亞國王迷宮的結構是否曾經存在過。換句話說，重建的建築 "看起來很真實"，但並不能 "準確地代表原來的克諾索斯"。

Again in "Knossos", the contributors of the New World Encyclopedia had also criticized how Evans mixed "old technology with new", and similar to the feeling of German at the end of the first paragraph in this section, the "complete reconstruction of sites does not correspond to the ideals of preservation".[15]

又在《克諾索斯》文中，《新世界百科全書》的撰稿人又批評埃文斯將"舊技術與新技術混為一談"，與本節第一段結尾 German 的感受類似，即"完全重建古蹟確實不符合保存的理想"。

(IV) Conclusion（結語）

Based on the above viewpoints, I believe my two confusions stated at the beginning of the introduction section have been assuredly answered. It is because:

基於以上觀點，我相信我在引言部分開頭所說的兩個困惑得到了肯定的解答。這是因為：

For my first confusion whether Evans' extensive pouring of concrete onto Knossos is the right way, the answer from German and New World Encyclopedia contributors is negative. It is because Evans' reconstruction approach to restore Knossos was destructive and irreversible, against the most important rule in restoring archaeological site in general.

對於我的第一個困惑，即埃文斯在克諾索斯上大量澆築混凝土是否是正確的方法，German 和《新世界百科全書》撰稿人的回答是否定的。這是因為埃文斯恢復克諾索斯的重建方法具有破壞性和不可逆轉性，違背了恢復考古遺址的最重要規則。

For my second confusion, as all three articles by German, Gere, and New World Encyclopedia contributors have questioned the accuracy of Evans' interpretation of Minoan civilization and architecture. Thus, unable to tell which parts of Evan's contribution are not true, Kostof is correct to allow only one sentence (total 11 words) to Evans' "spectacular digging" at Knossos.

對於我的第二個困惑，由於 German、Gere,、和《新世界百科全書》撰稿人的三篇文章都質疑埃文斯對米諾斯文明和建築的解釋的準確性，因此無法判斷埃文斯貢獻的哪些部分是不真實的，Kostof 只花了一句話（共 11 個字）來描寫埃文斯在克諾索斯"壯觀的挖掘"是正確的做法。

Notes

1. Moffat, Fazio, and Wodehouse, *A World History of Architecture 3rd Edition* (London: Laurence King Publishing Ltd, 2013), 34.

2. Kostof, Spiro, *A History of Architecture: Settings and Rituals 2nd Edition* (New York: Oxfird University Press, Inc., 1995), 107-8

3. German, Senta, "The Palace at Knossos (Crete)" in Smarthistory, July 11, 2018. https://smarthistory.org/ancient-mediterranean/the-palace-at-knossos-crete (accessed October 1, 2019).

4. Gere, Cathy, "The introduction to Knossos and the Prophets of Modernism" in *Knossos and the Prophets of Modernism* (Chicago: The University of Chicago

Press, 2009), 1-13.

https://www.press.uchicago.edu/Misc/Chicago/289533.html

(accessed September 27, 2019).

5. New World Encyclopedia contributors, "Knossos," New World Encyclopedia,

https://www.newworldencyclopedia.org/p/index.php?title=Knossos&oldid=1010925

(accessed September 27, 2019).

6. Mark, Joshua J. "Knossos," Ancient History Encyclopedia, last modified October 15, 2010.

https://www.ancient.eu/knossos/

(accessed September 26, 2019).

7. New World Encyclopedia contributors, "Knossos," 1.

8. German, "The Palace at Knossos (Crete), " 3-4.

9. Ibid., 5.

10. Ibid., 8.

11. Gere, "The introduction to Knossos and the Prophets of Modernism," 2.

12. Ibid.

13. Ibid., 1.

14. New World Encyclopedia contributors, "Knossos," 3.

15. Ibid.

書　　　　名	歐遊記快
作　　　　者	何大文
出　　　　版	超媒體出版有限公司
地　　　　址	荃灣柴灣角街 34-36 號萬達來工業中心 21 樓 2 室
出版計劃查詢	(852)3596 4296
電　　　　郵	info@easy-publish.org
網　　　　址	http://www.easy-publish.org
香 港 總 經 銷	聯合新零售 (香港) 有限公司
出 版 日 期	2023 年 11 月
圖 書 分 類	流行讀物
國 際 書 號	978-988-8839-39-1
定　　　　價	HK$75

Printed and Published in Hong Kong
版權所有‧侵害必究

如發現本書有釘裝錯漏問題，請攜同書刊親臨本公司服務部更換。